The Lonely Little Bear

For Ellie Roach – A.M.

For Tony – G.W.

Published in 1993 by Magi Publications
in association with Star Books International, 55 Crowland Avenue, Hayes, Middx UB3 4JP

Typeset by Impressions Bureau, London
Printed and Bound in Belgium by Proost N.V. Turnhout
ISBN 1 85430 255 8

The Lonely Little Bear

Written by
Anne Mangan
Illustrated by
Gwyneth Williamson

Magi Publications, London

There was once a little polar bear who wanted a home. He had lived for ages in a toy-shop, and when the Sales were over he was put right up on the top shelf to make way for the new toys. He sat between a yellow monkey and a big doll.

SALE
SALE
LAS
WEE

“The longer you are in the shop the higher you go,” whispered the monkey. “We’re all forgotten now. Children look on the low shelves.”

“Why wasn’t I sold?” asked the polar bear.
“Wrong shape,” said the monkey. “You look like a teddy, but you’re not a teddy-bear. You’re a polar bear. I’ve not been sold because I’m too yellow.”
“And I’m too expensive,” said the big doll.

"Cheer up! We can see lots of things from here," said the big doll, looking down. The little polar bear tried to look down into the shop, but felt dizzy. A shop wasn't like a home, he thought.

closed

“Bet I get sold tomorrow,” said the monkey.
He had a plan, and it worked. The next day he managed to fall off the shelf, right into a child’s arms.
“You could do that,” said the doll.
“I’d be too afraid,” said the little polar bear.
“I daren’t either,” said the doll. “I would break.”
So the big beautiful doll and the little polar bear sat side by side and waited and hoped . . .

A lady and her little girl came into the shop.
"We want something that's different," said the lady.
The little polar bear's heart lifted. He was certainly different.
The shop assistant reached up and took him down off the high shelf.
"He looks like a mistake," said the lady rudely.
"People would think we got him cheap."
They chose a calculator instead.
The little polar bear felt his insides sagging. It was awful to be a mistake. He flopped right over, and someone picked him up, gave him a shake and set him back in his place.

The next day a teenager came into the shop. She wanted a pretty toy to sit in her room and look nice. She saw the doll on the high shelf.

“Exactly what I’ve been looking for,” she said.
The big doll was overjoyed. She didn’t want to be hugged and loved as the little polar bear did. She just wanted to look pretty.

The little polar bear missed her dreadfully. He wanted a home more than ever. He sat there all alone, wishing and wishing . . .

The very next day it seemed as though his wish was granted, for a lady came into the shop. “What a jolly little bear,” she said, looking up. “I’ll have him for my youngest.” The little bear was delighted. He didn’t mind being bumped along in a bag all the way home.

Toy Shop

“I’ve a lovely surprise for you!” the lady told her small girl. “Look!”
“Ugh!” said the child. “I don’t want a silly bear. I want a racing car, you know I do.”
She threw the little bear across the room. Her mother picked him up. “I’ll change him for a car, shall I?”

The little polar bear was bumped all the way back to the shop, and put up on the high shelf again. He felt worse than ever. He had given up all hope of ever being wanted and loved.

One day a tall man and his wife came into the shop.
They had cheerful red faces.
"We'd like to buy a present for our niece," said the woman.
"A doll?" asked the shop assistant.
"Well, I don't know if she likes dolls," said the man.
"Some do and some don't."
The man was so tall that he could see the high shelf easily.

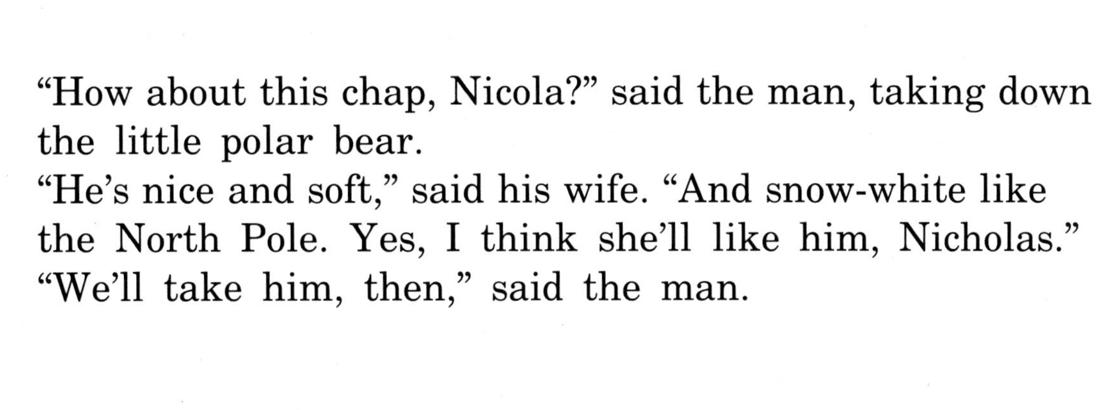

"How about this chap, Nicola?" said the man, taking down the little polar bear.
"He's nice and soft," said his wife. "And snow-white like the North Pole. Yes, I think she'll like him, Nicholas."
"We'll take him, then," said the man.

The little polar bear felt happy and afraid, all at the same time. He was worried that he'd be taken back to the shop again. Suppose their niece doesn't like me, he thought. Suppose she thinks I'm a mistake? Suppose she doesn't want a nice, white polar bear? The little bear worried and worried as they travelled along on the bus.

He worried again as they walked up the path to their niece's home. Suppose she wants a toy car instead?

A little girl opened the door. "Uncle Nicholas!" she said. "Aunt Nicola!"
"We've come with a special surprise, Eleanor," said Uncle Nicholas.
"You'll never guess what it is," said Aunt Nicola.
"Is it a doll?" asked Eleanor.
"*Barely* a doll," smiled Aunt Nicola, as Uncle Nicholas took the little polar bear from behind his back.
"Ooh," said Eleanor. She took the little bear and hugged him. She buried her face into his soft fur.
"*Thank you*," she said. "He's the nicest present I've ever had. I'll call you Nicky," she told the little bear. "After Aunt Nicola and Uncle Nicholas."

Now the little bear had a home and a name and someone who gave him lots and lots of hugs.
He was the happiest little polar bear in the world.